MW01096590

Many people live on my block.
They come from many places.

Tim's family came from China.

Sometimes they eat rice
and sometimes they eat pizza.

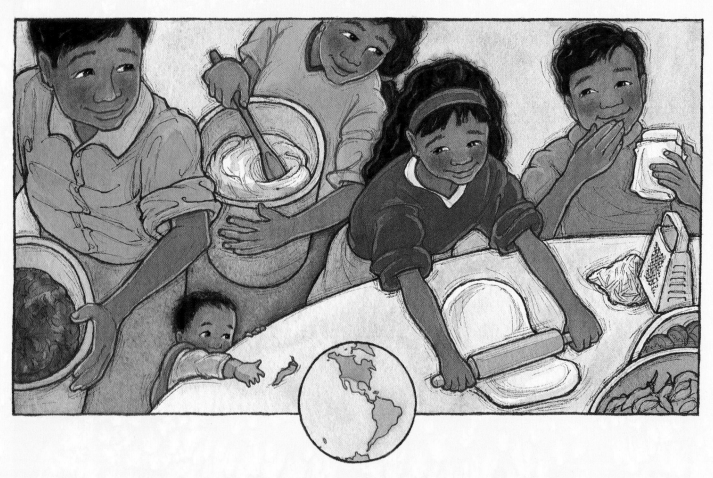

Monica's family came from Mexico.

Sometimes they eat burritos
and sometimes they eat pizza.

Christina's family came from India.

Sometimes they eat curry
and sometimes they eat pizza.

Joey's family came from Kenya.

Sometimes they eat cornmeal
and sometimes they eat pizza.

Mike's family came from Vietnam.

Sometimes they eat noodles
and sometimes they eat pizza.

Max's family came from Germany.

Sometimes they eat sausages
and sometimes they eat pizza.

Today is a special day.

We are having a block party.
Everyone is bringing food to eat.

We will all eat rice, burritos, curry, cornmeal, noodles, and sausages.

Who ordered the pizza?